THE SUPERSONIC SUBMARINE

JACK'S MEGA MACHINES
THE SUPERSONIC SUBMARINE

Alison Ritchie and Mike Byrne

SIMON AND SCHUSTER
London   New York   Sydney   Toronto   New Delhi

At the magical Rally Road workshop, Mechanic Jack was busy repairing a submarine. Jack was a brilliant mechanic – he could mend anything!

He straightened the periscope, welded the propeller and checked for leaks. A submarine has to be watertight!

Jack couldn't wait to try it out. He wondered what adventures his magic workshop would send him on this time!

Riley hopped in beside him and Jack shut the hatch.

SSHWOOSH!

The doors opened and the submarine glided out . . .

"Wow!" gasped Jack. He steered the now sleek and speedy submarine quickly through the water. He noticed some shadowy shapes bobbing about on the surface.

"I wonder what they are, Riley," said Jack. "Come on, let's go up and take a look!"

When they had nearly reached the surface, Jack peered through the periscope.

"Gosh! Dolphins – and lots of them! Looks like they want to talk to us."
Jack opened the submarine's hatch and climbed out.

"We need your help!" said the dolphins. "The giant octopus has snatched our football and we're in the middle of a match! He lives at the bottom of the sea, and we can't dive down that far."

"Leave it to me," said Jack.

Jack put the submarine into dive mode and slowly descended deeper and deeper, right to the bottom of the sea.

"Let's look in there!" said Jack, spotting a huge forest of seaweed.

Jack turned on the searchlights and
activated the sonar. He didn't want
to bump into anything in the dark!

He skilfully guided the submarine through the seaweed forest.
When they reached the middle, an amazing sight met their eyes . . .

a pirate shipwreck!

"Hey! What was that?" said Jack.

Jack steered the sub into the wreck and switched the beams onto high.

"I'm sure that was the giant octopus!" said Jack.

He and Riley searched every nook and cranny of the wreck.

They were about to give up when a huge shape shot past them – carrying a football! It zoomed out into the open sea.

Jack activated the radar. Ping! Ping! Ping! it went,
as it detected the octopus trying to get away.

"Time to go supersonic," said Jack, and pressed the red button.

They zoomed through the water. Whoosh!

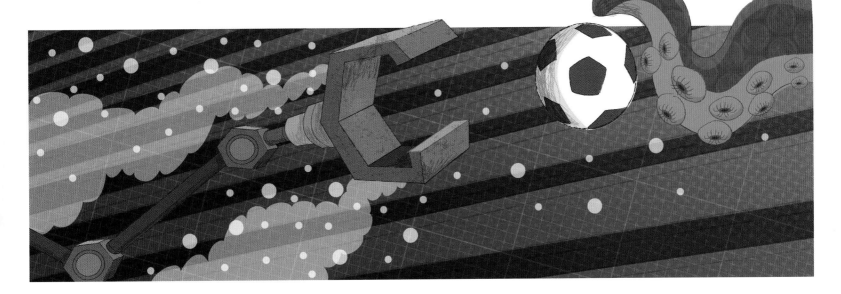

They were almost close enough to make a grab for the ball when . . .

. . . the octopus squirted a great cloud of ink into the water!

Jack couldn't see a thing and
the submarine was heading for a
jagged rock at top speed.
Suddenly . . .

. . . the submarine jolted backwards. The giant octopus had caught it and stopped it from crashing! "You need the ball, don't you?" asked the octopus.

"I'm sorry I took it. I just wanted to practise so I could play with the others!" he said.

"Well, you saved us in the nick of time," said Jack. "And that gives me an idea."

"You'll be the best goalie ever," said Jack.
"Just think of all the saves you'll be able to make now!
Three cheers for Octopus!"

All too soon it was time to go home.

"Come and see us again," said the dolphins. "We've got a match against the sharks, and with Octopus we might just win!"

"We'd love to," said Jack.

Then he and Riley waved goodbye and sped back to Rally Road.

"What an amazing undersea adventure," said Jack. "This sub really is supersonic, but I'm glad to be back on dry land. Come on, let's have a game of footy."

"Woof!" barked Riley, and got ready to make a supersonic save!

To Ygraine

– AR

For Archie

– MB

SIMON AND SCHUSTER

First published in Great Britain in 2013 by Simon and Schuster UK Ltd

1st Floor, 222 Gray's Inn Road, London WC1X 8HB

A CBS Company

Text copyright © 2013 Alison Ritchie

Illustrations copyright © 2013 Mike Byrne

Paper engineering by Maggie Bateson

Concept © 2012 Simon and Schuster UK

The right of Alison Ritchie and Mike Byrne to be identified

as the author and illustrator of this work has been asserted by them

in accordance with the Copyright, Designs and Patents Act, 1988

A CIP catalogue record for this book is available from the British Library upon request

ISBN: 978-0-85707-569-7

eBook ISBN: 978-0-85707-891-9

Printed in China

1 3 5 7 9 10 8 6 4 2

**Look out for more of
Jack's amazing adventures
in a bookshop near you!**

**Jack's Mega Machines:
The Rocket Racing Car**

**Jack's Mega Machines:
The Dinosaur Digger**

**Jack's Mega Machines:
The Mighty Monster Truck**

HAVE FUN WITH JACK IN HIS MEGA MACHINES!

In this underwater adventure, Jack dives into a football match. Can he help the dolphins find their ball at the bottom of the ocean or will he meet a deep water danger?

Look out for more adventures with Jack and his mega machines!

CE Warning! Not s... ...ldren under 36 mont... ...ll parts

KR-904-945

ISBN 978-0-857075-569-7

£6.99
www.simonandschuster.co.uk

9 780857 075697